W9-BJS-327

Dear Parents:

Congratulations! Your child is taking the first steps on an exciting journey. The destination? Independent reading!

STEP INTO READING® will help your child get there. The program offers five steps to reading success. Each step includes fun stories and colorful art or photographs. In addition to original fiction and books with favorite characters, there are Step into Reading Non-Fiction Readers, Phonics Readers and Boxed Sets, Sticker Readers, and Comic Readers—a complete literacy program with something to interest every child.

Learning to Read, Step by Step!

Ready to Read   Preschool–Kindergarten
• big type and easy words • rhyme and rhythm • picture clues
For children who know the alphabet and are eager to begin reading.

Reading with Help   Preschool–Grade 1
• basic vocabulary • short sentences • simple stories
For children who recognize familiar words and sound out new words with help.

Reading on Your Own   Grades 1–3
• engaging characters • easy-to-follow plots • popular topics
For children who are ready to read on their own.

Reading Paragraphs   Grades 2–3
• challenging vocabulary • short paragraphs • exciting stories
For newly independent readers who read simple sentences with confidence.

Ready for Chapters   Grades 2–4
• chapters • longer paragraphs • full-color art
For children who want to take the plunge into chapter books but still like colorful pictures.

STEP INTO READING® is designed to give every child a successful reading experience. The grade levels are only guides; children will progress through the steps at their own speed, developing confidence in their reading.

Remember, a lifetime love of reading starts with a single step!

Step into Reading, Random House, and the Random House colophon are registered trademarks of Penguin Random House LLC.

Visit us on the Web!
StepIntoReading.com
rhcbooks.com

Educators and librarians, for a variety of teaching tools, visit us at RHTeachersLibrarians.com

ISBN 978-0-593-37343-9 (trade) — ISBN 978-0-593-37344-6 (lib. bdg.)
ISBN 978-0-593-37345-3 (ebook)

Printed in the United States of America

10 9 8 7 6 5 4 3 2 1

DREAMWORKS

Trolls

Tiny Diamond's First Day of School

by David Lewman

illustrated by Fabio Laguna and Grace Mills

Random House 🏠 New York

Guy Diamond wakes
his son, Tiny Diamond.
Today is the first day
of school!
Tiny Diamond is
still a little sleepy.

On the way to school,
Tiny and his daddy
meet Queen Poppy.

She tells
Tiny Diamond
that he will make
new friends fast!

At school,
there are lots
of young Trolls.

Suddenly, Tiny Diamond
feels shy.
But he will try hard
to make friends.

The teacher tells
the students that
they will learn
lots of new things.

"Who likes bubbles?"

she asks.

Tiny wants to blow
the biggest bubble.
But he gets stuck
inside one!

The teacher says
they should work together
to paint a picture.
But Tiny makes
his own big picture.

At story time,
Tiny Diamond wants
to tell a story.
The teacher says
it is time to listen.

At playtime,

Tiny starts to dance.

He kicks up a lot of dust.

"Ahhh—"

"—CHOO!"

When Tiny sneezes, glitter flies everywhere!

The teacher tells
the students to sneeze
into their elbows.

At snack time,
Tiny Diamond
wants a cupcake!
First they all have
to wash their hands.

Tiny Diamond is sad.

He is not making friends.

But at music time,

he knows what to do!

Tiny raps!
*"I love to rap
in any weather!
But music is better
when we make it together!"*

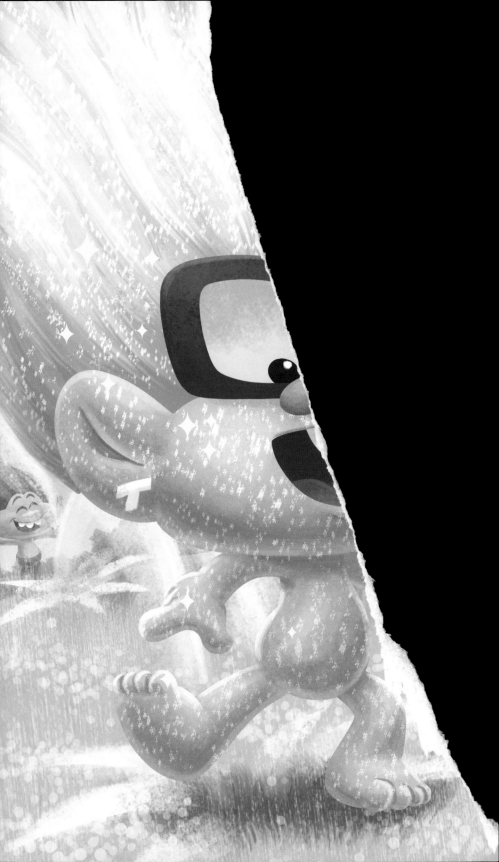

he other Trolls make up
their own rhymes.

Everyone loves rapping.

They all become friends!

Tiny Diamond is happy.
He has made new friends,
and his teacher is cool.
TINY DIAMOND
LOVES SCHOOL!